Don't tell lies, Lucy!

A cautionary tale

Phil Roxbee Cox

Illustrated by Jan McCafferty

Edited by Jenny Tyler
Designed by Non Figg

First published in 2004 by Usborne Publishing Ltd., 83-85 Saffron Hill, London, EC1N 8RT www.usborne.com
Copyright © 2004 Usborne Publishing Limited. The name Usborne and the devices ♀⊕ are Trade Marks of Usborne Publishing Ltd.
All rights reserved. No part of this publication may be reproduced, stored in a retrieval system, or transmitted in any form or by
any means, electronic, mechanical, photocopy, recording or otherwise, without prior permission of the publisher.
First published in America in 2004. UE. Printed in Dubai.

This is Lucy.

Lucy often tells lies.

Once, Lucy tore her T-shirt.

4

"I was kidnapped by pirates!" she cried.

"Don't tell lies, Lucy!"
Lucy's mother sadly sighed.

Once, Lucy broke a window.

Once, Lucy made a big 'SPLASH!'

Once, Lucy did some drawing
on her bedroom wall.

Lucy's borrowed Paul's bike.

She rides into a tree.

"It wasn't my fault, Paul.
A bandit *jumped* in front of me!"

Paul runs off angrily to find their family.

13

"There'll be no more lying, Lucy!

We can't take it anymore!"

"But I'm *not* lying," Lucy lies.
She stomps her foot upon the floor.

She runs from room...

to room...

to room...

slamming every door.

While Lucy's sulking on her bed

and told she *must* behave...

"Everybody out!"
shouts Dad.

"A HUGE WAVE
is on the way."

18

The others hurry through the door...

...but Lucy's going to stay.

"You are lying, Dad," she shouts.

"I don't believe a word you say!"

Which is how the
GREAT BIG WAVE COMES...

...to wash Lucy far away.

"That's the trouble
with those who lie,"
Dad says to Auntie Bea.

"They think the
rest of us lie too."

"Anyone for tea?"